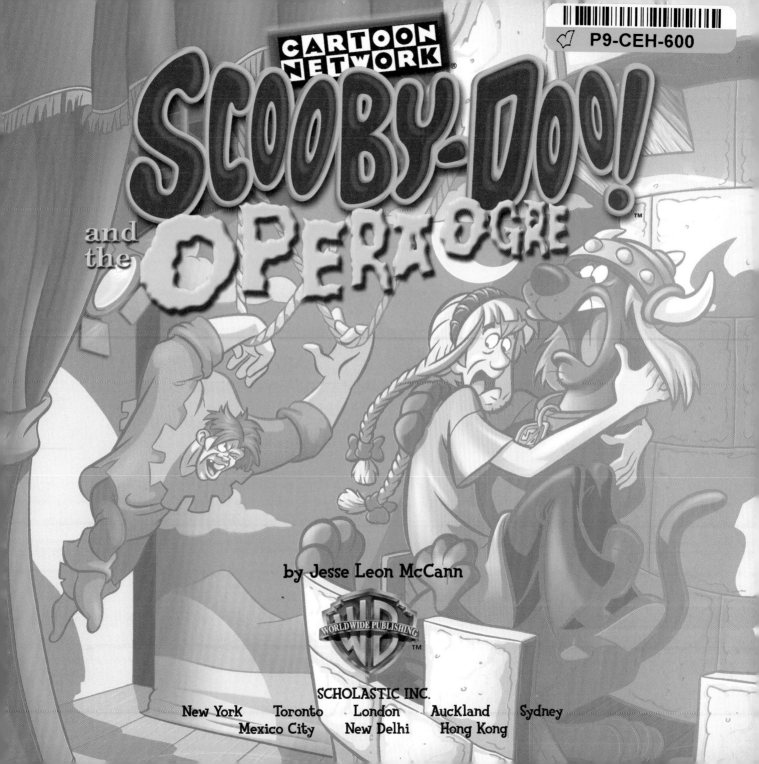

CARTOON NETWORK®

SCOOBY-DOO!

and the OPERA OGRE

by Jesse Leon McCann

WORLDWIDE PUBLISHING

SCHOLASTIC INC.

New York   Toronto   London   Auckland   Sydney
Mexico City   New Delhi   Hong Kong

In loving memory of my aunt, Loretta Kennedy, who took me to my first musical.

ISBN 0-439-26074-4

Designed by Louise Bova

12 11 10 9 8 7 6 5 4   2 3 4 5 6/0

Special thanks to Duendes del Sur for
cover and interior illustrations.
Printed in the U.S.A.
First Scholastic printing, April 2001

"Awr-roooooo!" howled Scooby-Doo.

"And, like, la-la-la-la Figaro! Figaro! Figaro!" sang Shaggy.

"All right, you two," Daphne scolded them. "Just because we're going to the opera doesn't mean *you* have to sing!"

Sure enough, the Mystery Machine was pulling up to a fancy theater. But it looked like the opera house was on fire!

"Gee, what's going on here?" Velma asked as the gang climbed out of the Mystery Machine.

"Oh, it's terrible!" cried Mr. Samuels, the owner of the opera house. "Our entire production is ruined!"

All around Mr. Samuels, people were running out of the smoking opera house. There were audience members in fancy clothes, musicians in tuxedos, stage technicians all dressed in black, and performers in Viking costumes.

Mr. Samuels told Scooby and the gang what had happened. "The audience was enjoying our debut production of *The Viking Voyage* when all of a sudden, a strange creature swung down from the rafters. He was carrying a torch in his hand, and he lit the stage on fire! There was smoke everywhere, and everyone panicked and ran for the exits!"

"Oh, my goodness! Is everyone okay?" asked Velma.

"Yes, I think so," replied Mr. Samuels. "Except for one person — the star of the opera, Paul Noble! He's missing!"

One of the singers, a man named William Bluster, approached Mr. Samuels. "Don't worry, Samuels," Bluster said. "I can play the lead part. I am an expert in all things theatrical!" With a sniff he added, "Paul Noble probably went home. He's such a coward."

Mr. Samuels didn't know what to do. It was all so confusing. Then the firemen came out of the opera house looking puzzled.

There was no fire inside! Just a lot of smoke.

"Mr. Samuels, do you mind if we take a look inside?" Fred asked. "We're pretty good at solving mysteries like this."

Mr. Samuels was glad for the help. So the gang went inside, eager to find the cause of all the trouble. (Actually, Scooby and Shaggy were hoping to find a snack bar.)

No sooner had they entered the grand theater than a creepy shadow appeared onstage.

"*Stay away!* Beware!" the shadow screamed. "Beware the wrath of the opera ogre!"

"Zoinks!" Shaggy cried. He and Scooby were so scared, they jumped into the orchestra pit. Shaggy ended up leaping headfirst into a big tuba.

"Like, help! I'm blind!" Shaggy hollered.

"Stop fooling around, you two," Velma chided.

Then something strange happened. When Scooby looked up at the gang from the orchestra pit, he realized that he was going *down* — and so was the whole pit!

The orchestra pit worked just like a big elevator! Normally it took the orchestra up to the stage level. Now it took Shaggy and Scooby down to a dark place under the stage, where sets and props were kept.

"Like, wow, Scoob! I'll bet most people don't get to see this area," Shaggy said. "Let's look around!"

"Ruh-ruh!" Scooby shook his head. "Rit's roo rooky!"

"Too spooky?" Shaggy exclaimed. "No way, Scoob! Look, there are the dressing rooms. I'll bet the performers get all sorts of goodies, like fruit baskets and boxes of chocolates!"

"Rhocolates?" Scooby changed his mind. "Ret's ro!"

Scooby and Shaggy went into a dressing room with a gold star on the door. It belonged to the show's star, Paul Noble.

"Groovy, Scoob!" exclaimed Shaggy.

Scooby couldn't agree more. He sat at the makeup table and pretended he was a famous stage actor. He laughed at his reflection. "Ree-hee-hee!"

"Like, let's see what's in the closet," Shaggy said. Then he got a big scare!

Rrrrrmmmm! said the creature inside, reaching for Shaggy.

"Zoinks! It's a mummy!" Shaggy shouted.

Meanwhile, Fred, Daphne, and Velma were exploring the stage area. Off to the side of the main stage area was a place the audience couldn't see, called the "wings."

"This is where they keep the set pieces until they're ready to go onstage," Daphne explained. "And see those ropes? Those are used to raise and lower the scenery."

The kids were so busy looking at the scenery, they didn't see the creepy shadow of the opera ogre behind them on the floor — until it was too late!

Ka-boom! There was a fiery explosion, then out jumped the opera ogre!

"So! You have intruded on my domain, despite my warnings," the ogre said, his eyes glittering. "Now you must face my wrath!"

"Jinkies!" Velma exclaimed. "Let's get out of here! Exit stage left!"

Fred, Daphne, and Velma ran as fast as their feet could carry them! But before they got far, the ogre recited an eerie poem:

"Fire burn and cauldron bubble!
Bring forth my Viking warriors, on the double!"

Suddenly, Fred and the girls were surrounded by an army of ghostlike Vikings, all grinning evilly!

The kids tried to get away, but they took a wrong turn.

"Jeepers!" Daphne shuddered. "This brings new meaning to the phrase 'stage fright'!"

"There's something strange about these Vikings," Velma remarked. "And we're going to get to the bottom of it."

Velma sounded brave, but it was hard not to shiver as the eerie Viking army crept closer!

In another part of the theater, the mummy was chasing Shaggy and Scooby. The two friends ran through the theater's green room with the mummy hot on their tail. Every big theater has a green room. It's the area where actors meet with audience members after a performance. Usually it's a very pleasant place to be. But right then, Scooby and Shaggy didn't find it pleasant at all! The mummy was gaining on them!

Luckily, Shaggy and Scooby were able to pull the old "one-two" on the mummy. The growling creature soon found itself sliding down a laundry chute.

"Like, make sure you use plenty of starch!" Shaggy called down the chute after the mummy.

Scooby got a big laugh out of that. Then he caught a glimpse of something exciting out of the corner of his eye!

"Rook, Raggy!" Scooby pointed.

COSTUME LAUNDRY CHUTE

It was the costume room!

Shaggy and Scooby couldn't resist. They had to try on some costumes.

There were costumes of Kings, soldiers, cowboys, princesses, witches, and vampires!

"Like, we sure could have used disguises like these on some of our adventures!" Shaggy said as he dressed up as a fairy-tale princess. "Right, Scoob?"

"Ruh-huh!" Scooby agreed wholeheartedly, prancing around like a Roman general in battle.

Meanwhile, Fred, Daphne, and Velma were realizing something.

"Those Vikings haven't moved any closer," said Velma.

"And the opera ogre has disappeared!" Daphne added.

"Look!" exclaimed Fred. "These Vikings aren't ghosts after all. They're just big puppets."

The opera ogre had fooled the kids into thinking they were surrounded! Now he was off to cause mischief elsewhere in the theater.

"C'mon, guys." Fred was heading offstage. "Let's see if we can't catch up with that tricky fellow!"

The kids soon found themselves in one of the dressing rooms. It was a big, long room where the chorus actors got ready before the show.

Daphne found a picture of the star, Paul Noble. Someone had drawn a funny face on it. "Boy, someone sure can't stand Paul Noble," she commented.

"Look at this. It could be a clue!" Velma exclaimed. She pointed at a container filled with smoke-making fluid used for special effects.

"And I found these long strips of canvas." Fred frowned. "What are these doing in the actors' dressing room?"

BLUSTER — UNDERSTUDY

SMOKE MACHINE FLUID

Upstairs, Shaggy and Scooby had run into a problem — an ogre of a problem!

Right in the middle of their play-acting, the opera ogre leaped into the costume room with a loud laugh.

"Flee now, or feel the wrath of the opera ogre!" he whispered menacingly.

"Zoinks! No need for wrath-ing, today, Mr. Creepy!" Shaggy cried as he and Scooby fled the room. "We're fleeing! We're fleeing!"

Scooby and Shaggy ran out to an area overlooking the stage. They came to a circular staircase used by the stage crew, and up they went. The opera ogre was close behind!

When Shaggy and Scooby got to the top of the staircase, they came to a locked door. It was a dead end!

"Like, only one way to go, Scoob!" Shaggy pointed to a pole that had a scenery backdrop tied to it. "I hope you're good at hand-over-hand crawling."

Scooby gulped as he peered down at the approaching ogre. "Ri ram row!"

Just as the ogre reached the top of the stairs, Shaggy and Scooby jumped onto the scenery pole. They started climbing away.

But the ogre didn't follow. Instead, he grinned and cut the support rope that was holding up the backdrop!

Down, down, down Shaggy and Scooby fell — and fast!

"Good-bye, Scoob, old pal!" Shaggy sniffled. "Like, it looks like splatsville for us!"

"Roh-roh-roh!" Scooby cried.

Then, a miraculous thing happened. Scooby-Doo and Shaggy hit the sail of the Viking boat onstage. The silk of the sail acted like a slide. They glided smoothly toward the bottom!

"Now *that's* more like it," cheered Shaggy.

"Reah! Reah!" Scooby nodded happily.

But just when they thought they were going to get away, free and clear . . .

"Rrrrrmmm!"

"Zoinks!" Shaggy exclaimed. "It's that funky mummy at the bottom of the sail! And it's reaching for us, Scoob!"

The mummy did, indeed, seem to reaching for them. But when they reached the bottom, the mummy didn't grab them. Instead, the two buddies accidentally kicked the mummy and sent it flying!

Shaggy laughed. "How about that?"

Scooby grinned. "Reah, row arout rat?"

Daphne, Fred, and Velma heard the commotion onstage. So they ran back out to see what was happening.

"Look!" Velma pointed. "There's a mummy chasing Shaggy and Scooby!"

"Let's help them!" Fred said.

The kids started toward Shaggy and Scooby. But before they could get very far . . .

Splat! The opera ogre was cutting heavy sandbags loose overhead, trying to hit the gang.

"Jeepers! It's too dangerous!" Daphne cried. "Get back!"

Shaggy and Scooby were having problems of
their own. The mummy chased them into the
scenery shop behind the stage. This was the place
where the sets were designed, built, and painted.

Crash! Shaggy ran into some old paint cans.

Smash! Scooby skidded into a stack of lumber.

They were so busy running into things, they
didn't realize that the mummy was as clumsy as
they were.

Bash! The mummy hit its head on a post.

Dashing through the falling sandbags, the rest of the gang joined Shaggy and Scooby in the scenery shop.

"Jinkies! What's all the noise in here?" Velma wondered.

"Like, that crazy mummy is trying to grab us and put one of its creepy curses on us!" Shaggy said.

"Reah, reepy rurses!" Scooby nodded.

"Well, I don't think this mummy can do much to you guys right now," Fred said, examining the unconscious mummy. "It's out cold!"

Just then, Velma made an interesting discovery.

"Hey, look!" she exclaimed. "It's not a real torch at all! It's just a prop made from cellophane and wood, with a tiny light and fan inside!"

"And this is a machine that makes artificial fog and smoke," said Fred. "I think I know what's been going on here."

The kids began to realize that everything was not what it seemed onstage. In fact, Shaggy and Scooby found that out the hard way when they bit into some legs of lamb made out of painted foam!

"Well, two can play at that game," Fred said. "Listen, gang. I've got an idea. . . ."

A short time later, Shaggy and Scooby were back onstage. They were pretending to be Romeo and Juliet.

"I sure hope this works," Shaggy said nervously.

"Rhat right rhough ronder rindow reaks?" Scooby said to Shaggy, playing along.

But the ploy worked. For, just then, the opera ogre appeared, swinging down to get them — just like they wanted!

"Defy me, will you?" growled the ogre. "Very well. You can't escape me now!"

"Zoinks! That's our cue, Scoob!" Shaggy yelled. "Like, let's get out of here!"

The opera ogre chased Shaggy and Scooby off the stage and into one of the hallways.

"Relp! Relp!" Scooby cried.

"Like, just keep running, Scoob!" Shaggy huffed. "If we stop, he'll get us!"

"Oh, I'll get you, I will," sneered the ogre. "And your little dog, too!"

Just when it looked like the ogre was going to nab them for sure, Shaggy and Scooby veered suddenly to one side.

Before the ogre could change direction, he smashed through a canvas wall. He didn't notice it because it was painted to look just like the hallway!

Fred was waiting on the other side. When the ogre crashed through, Fred tied him up as neat as you please!

"Like, that's one snazzy special effect!" Shaggy laughed.

"Ruh-huh!" Scooby agreed.

"Now let's see who this opera ogre really is." Fred ripped off the ogre's mask. "It's that actor, William Bluster!"

"And the mummy is the missing star, Paul Noble!" Daphne exclaimed. "He wasn't trying to get us. He was just asking us to help untie him!"

"I'll bet Bluster kidnapped him," Velma added.

"Yeah! And with Paul Noble out of the way, they would've let me play his part!" growled William Bluster. "The plan would've worked, too, if it weren't for you nosy kids and your dog!"

Just then, Mr. Samuels ran in with the police to take Bluster away.

"Thanks for solving the mystery, kids!" Mr. Samuels said. "What can I do to repay you?"

"Well, there *is* one thing." Shaggy smiled at Scooby.

"Reah! Reah!" said Scooby excitedly.

Later, the audience was back in their seats. The opera began with Paul Noble in the lead, just where he belonged. Only now there were two new members in the Viking chorus — Scooby and Shaggy!

"Like, this is the grooviest reward of all!" Shaggy said.

And even in the last row, you could hear Scooby loud and clear when he sang out, "Scooby-Dooby-Doo!"